Lots of Limericks

EDITED BY MYRA COHN LIVINGSTON

DILLY DILLY PICCALILLI:
POEMS FOR THE VERY YOUNG

IF THE OWL CALLS AGAIN:
A COLLECTION OF OWL POEMS

I LIKE YOU, IF YOU LIKE ME:
POEMS OF FRIENDSHIP

POEMS OF CHRISTMAS

WHY AM I GROWN SO COLD?
POEMS OF THE UNKNOWABLE
(Margaret K. McElderry Books)

HOW PLEASANT TO KNOW MR. LEAR!

POEMS OF LEWIS CARROLL

THESE SMALL STONES

ALSO BY MYRA COHN LIVINGSTON

HIGGLEDY-PIGGLEDY:
VERSES AND PICTURES

MONKEY PUZZLE AND OTHER POEMS

REMEMBERING AND OTHER POEMS

THERE WAS A PLACE AND OTHER POEMS

WORLDS I KNOW AND OTHER POEMS
(Margaret K. McElderry Books)

BIRTHDAY POEMS

CELEBRATIONS

THE CHILD AS POET:
MYTH OR REALITY?

A CIRCLE OF SEASONS

CLIMB INTO THE BELL TOWER:
ESSAYS ON POETRY

EARTH SONGS

MY HEAD IS RED AND OTHER RHYMES

POEM-MAKING: WAYS TO BEGIN WRITING POETRY

SEA SONGS

SKY SONGS

A SONG I SANG TO YOU

SPACE SONGS

UP IN THE AIR

Lots of Limericks

Selected by Myra Cohn Livingston
Illustrated by Rebecca Perry

MARGARET K. MCELDERRY BOOKS
NEW YORK

MAXWELL MACMILLAN CANADA
TORONTO

MAXWELL MACMILLAN INTERNATIONAL
NEW YORK   OXFORD   SINGAPORE   SYDNEY

To Edmund, Charlotte, and Hannah Hoffman

Margaret K. McElderry Books
Macmillan Publishing Company
866 Third Avenue
New York, NY 10022

Maxwell Macmillan Canada, Inc.
1200 Eglinton Avenue East
Suite 200
Don Mills, Ontario M3C 3N1

Macmillan Publishing Company is part of the Maxwell Communication Group of Companies.

First edition
Printed in the United States of America
1 2 3 4 5 6 7 8 9 10

Library of Congress Cataloging-in-Publication Data
Lots of limericks / selected by Myra Cohn Livingston. — 1st ed.
p. cm.
Summary: A collection of limericks on such topics as accidents and incidents, peculiar people, strange shapes, and holidays.
ISBN 0-689-50531-0
1. Limericks, Juvenile. [1. Limericks. 2. American poetry—Collections. 3. English poetry—Collections.]
PN6231.L5L6 1991 91-329
821'.075'08—dc20

ACKNOWLEDGMENTS

The editor and publisher thank the following for permission to reprint the copyrighted material listed below. Every effort has been made to locate all persons having any rights or interests in the material published here. Any existing rights not here acknowledged will, if the editor or publisher is notified, be duly acknowledged in future editions of this book.

BRANDT & BRANDT LITERARY AGENTS, INC. for "Said an Ogre from Old Saratoga," from *A Seizure of Limericks* by Conrad Aiken. Copyright © 1963, 1964 by Conrad Aiken. Reprinted by permission of Brandt & Brandt Literary Agents, Inc.

CURTIS BROWN, LTD. for "A Bright Idea" and "Sticky Situation," from *The Phantom Ice Cream Man* by X. J. Kennedy. Copyright © 1975, 1977, 1978, 1979 by X. J. Kennedy. Reprinted by permission of Curtis Brown, Ltd.

JUDITH CIARDI for "There was a young fellow named Shear," by John Ciardi. Copyright © 1976.

DOUBLEDAY for "Philander," copyright © 1961, and "The Yak," copyright © 1952 by Theodore Roethke, from *The Collected Poems of Theodore Roethke* by Theodore Roethke. Used by permission of Doubleday, a division of Bantam Doubleday Dell Publishing Group, Inc.

FARRAR, STRAUS & GIROUX, INC. for "A matron well known in Montclair," "An obnoxious Old Person named Hackett," "An Old Man from Okefenokee," "There was a Young Lady named Rose," "There was a Young Person named Crockett," "There was an Old Lady named Crockett," "There was an Old Lady named Hart," and "There was an Old Man from Luray," from *Laughing Time* by William Jay Smith. Copyright © 1955, 1957, 1980, 1990 by William Jay Smith. Reprinted by permission of Farrar, Straus & Giroux, Inc.

EDWARD GOREY for "An impressionable lady in Wales," by Edward Gorey. Used with permission of the Children's Book Council. Originally appeared in *Limericks for Book Week, 1975*. Copyright © 1975. "From Number Nine, Penwiper Mews," copyright © 1978 by Edward Gorey.

HARPER & ROW, PUBLISHERS, INC. for "There was a sad pig with a tail," "There was a young pig from Chanute," and "There was a young pig who, in bed," (text only), from *The Book of Pigericks: Pig Limericks* by Arnold Lobel. Copyright © 1983 by Arnold Lobel. All selections reprinted by permission of Harper & Row, Publishers, Inc. "I wish that my room had a floor;" and "I'd rather have fingers than toes;" from *The Burgess Nonsense Book* by Gelett Burgess (J. B. Lippincott). "Young Frankenstein's robot invention," by Berton Braley, from *Laughable Limericks*, compiled by Sara and John Brewton (Harper & Row, 1965).

HOUGHTON MIFFLIN COMPANY for "April Fool," "Be Kind to Dumb Animals," "The Halloween House," "It Came from Outer Space," "Keeping Busy Is Better Than Nothing," "Sometimes Even Parents Win," "The Thinker," and "Win Some, Lose Some," from *The Hopeful Trout and Other Limericks* by John Ciardi. Text copyright © 1989 by Myra J. Ciardi. Reprinted by permission of Houghton Mifflin Company.

J. PATRICK LEWIS for "There once was a dancing black bear" (copyright © 1991), "Cries a sheep to a ship on the Amazon" (copyright © 1991), "There is a young reindeer named Donder" (copyright © 1984), and "A woman named Mrs. S. Claus" (copyright © 1984) by J. Patrick Lewis.

LITTLE, BROWN AND COMPANY for "A man who was fond of his skunk," "There once was a man in the Moon," "There once was a scarecrow named Joel," "There was a young man, let me say," and "This season our tunnips was red," from *One at a Time* by David McCord. Copyright © 1961, 1962 by David McCord. "There was an Old Man of Calcutta" and "A Bugler Named Dougal MacDougal," from *Primrose Path* by Ogden Nash. Copyright © 1935 by Ogden Nash. "The Pilgrims Ate Quahogs and Corn Yet," from *There's Always Another Windmill* by Ogden Nash. Copyright © 1967 by Ogden Nash; first appeared in *Holiday* as one of "Ten New Limericks." All selections reprinted by permission of Little, Brown and Company.

MACMILLAN PUBLISHING COMPANY for "My Sister," reprinted with permission of Margaret K. McElderry Books, an imprint of Macmillan Publishing Company, from *Nonstop Nonsense* by Margaret Mahy. Copyright © 1977 by Margaret Mahy. "On a day when the ocean was sharky," " 'Now just who,' muses Uncle Bill Biddle," and "A luckless time-traveler from Lynn," reprinted with permission of Margaret K. McElderry Books, an imprint of Macmillan Publishing Company, from *Ghastlies, Goops & Pincushions* by X. J. Kennedy. Copyright © 1989 by X. J. Kennedy. "Pitcher McDowell," "A Man in a Tree," "A Lady in Madrid," "A Driver from Deering," "A Person in Stirling," "A Man of Pennang," "A Person in Spain," "An Explorer Named Bliss," and "A Crusty Mechanic," reprinted with permission of Margaret K. McElderry Books, an imprint of Macmillan Publishing Company, from *A Person from Britain* by N. M. Bodecker. Copyright © 1980 by N. M. Bodecker.

THE NEW YORKER for "Said a lady beyond Compton Lakes," from "Limericks Long After Lear" by Morris Bishop. Reprinted by permission; © 1936, 1964 Alison K. Bishop. Originally in *The New Yorker*.

PENGUIN BOOKS LTD. for "There was a young fellow called Hugh" by Max Fatchen, from *Songs for My Dog and Other People* by Max Fatchen (Viking Kestrel, 1980), copyright © Max Fatchen, 1980.

JACK PRELUTSKY for "A silly young fellow named Ben," copyright © 1989 by Jack Prelutsky.

THE PUTNAM PUBLISHING GROUP for "Said a foolish young lady of Wales" by Langford Reed in *The Complete Limerick Book, 1925*. "Said old Peeping Tom of Fort Lee" by Morris Bishop in *Spilt Milk, 1942*. "Said Rev. Rectangular Square" by Clinton Brooks Burgess and "There once was a man who said, 'Why,'" in *Carolyn Wells' Book of American Limericks, 1925*.

RANDOM CENTURY GROUP for "Doctor Who, I am forced to admit," from *Versicles and Limericks* by Charles Connell (Hutchinson).

MARIAN REINER for "Said the monster," from *See My Lovely Poison Ivy* by Lilian Moore. Copyright © 1975 by Lilian Moore. Reprinted by permission of Marian Reiner for the author. "An Odd One," from "Animalimericks" in *Jamboree: Rhymes For All Times* by Eve Merriam. Copyright © 1962, 1964, 1966, 1973 by Eve Merriam. All rights reserved. Reprinted by permission of Marian Reiner for the author. "Tennis Clinic," from *The Sidewalk Racer and Other Poems of Sports and Motion* by Lillian Morrison. Copyright © 1965, 1967, 1968, 1977 by Lillian Morrison. Reprinted by permission of Marian Reiner for the author. "Fourth of July," from *Celebrations* by Myra Cohn Livingston. Copyright © 1985 by Myra Cohn Livingston. Holiday House, New York. Reprinted by permission of Marian Reiner for the author. "A discerning young lamb of Long Sutton," "A small mouse in Middleton Stoney," "Cried a man on the Salisbury Plain," "Said a restless young person of Yew," "There was once a young fellow of Wall," and "Wailed a ghost in a graveyard at Kew," from *A Lollygag of Limericks* by Myra Cohn Livingston. Copyright © 1978 by Myra Cohn Livingston. Reprinted by permission of Marian Reiner for the author.

ROTHCO CARTOONS for "There was a young lady named Bright" by A. H. Reginald Buller, and "A scientist living at Staines" by R. J. P. Hewison. Originally appeared in *Punch*. Copyright © Punch/Rothco.

THE SATURDAY EVENING POST SOCIETY for "A mathematician named Bath" by J. F. Wilson. Reprinted from *The Saturday Evening Post*, copyright © 1974.

WALLACE TRIPP for "Going home with her books through the snows," by Wallace Tripp. Used with permission of the Children's Book Council. Originally appeared in *Limericks for Book Week, 1975*. Copyright © 1975.

CONTENTS

INTRODUCTION 1

A BUNDLE OF BIRDBRAINS 3

INCIDENTS AND ACCIDENTS 15

PECULIAR PEOPLE 27

STRANGE SHAPES 41

ALL IN THE HEAD 51

FABULOUS FOODS 61

ODD NUMBERS AND OUTER SPACE 71

FLUTES AND FIDDLES 83

WORDPLAY AND PUNS 93

HAPPY HOLIDAYS 103

THE VERY END 109

INDEX OF AUTHORS 121

INDEX OF TITLES AND FIRST LINES 123

INTRODUCTION

Nobody really knows how the limerick began. Some say that it was a form of popular song sung by a brigade of Irish soldiers who returned from France to Limerick, Ireland, early in the eighteenth century. Others have found that the form appears in a Greek play written sometime between 448 and 380 B.C. and in manuscripts from the fourteenth and sixteenth centuries. A limerick even appears in Shakespeare's *Othello*.

We do know that the first book of limericks was published in England as *The History of Sixteen Wonderful Old Women* in 1821. The next year another book appeared in which a verse about a man of Tobago so inspired Edward Lear that, over fifty years later, he patterned his famous nonsense verses on the form. Lear has been called the Poet Laureate of the Limerick.

Today, the limerick is a light verse form which appeals to us through its ridiculous humor, its word-play, and its bouncing anapestic rhythm. Many of the limericks we know are anonymous, but a good many others are always appearing, some written by our best contemporary poets.

This is a selection of 210 of my favorite limericks, old and new, with the hope that you will find some that will also make you laugh, read, and even sing!

—MCL

A Bundle of Birdbrains

I wish that my room had a floor;
I don't care so much for a door;
    But this walking around
    Without touching the ground
Is getting to be quite a bore.

Gelett Burgess

THE GNAT AND THE GNU

"How absurd," said the gnat to the gnu,
"To spell your queer name as you do!"
    "For the matter of that,"
    Said the gnu to the gnat,
"That's just how I feel about you."

Oliver Herford

"This season our tunnips was red
And them beets was all white. And instead
    Of green cabbages, what
    You suspect that we got?"
"I don't know." "Didn't plant none," he said.

David McCord

There once was a boy of Bagdad,
An inquisitive sort of a lad.
    He said, "I will see
    If a sting has a bee."
And he very soon found that it had.

KEEPING BUSY IS BETTER THAN NOTHING

There was a young lady named Sue
Who had nothing whatever to do
    And who did it so badly
    I thought she would gladly
Have stopped long before she was through.

John Ciardi

There was a young bard of Japan
Whose limericks never would scan;
    When they said it was so,
    He replied: "Yes, I know,
But I make a rule of always trying to get
just as many words into the last line as
I possibly can."

There was a young fellow called Hugh
Who went to a neighbouring zoo.
    The lion opened wide
    And said, "Come inside
And bring all the family too."

Max Fatchen

THE THINKER

There was a young fellow who thought
Very little, but thought it a lot.
    Then at long last he knew
    What he wanted to do,
But before he could start, he forgot.

John Ciardi

There's a tiresome young man from Bay Shore;
When his fiancée cried, "I adore
    The beautiful sea!"
    He replied, "I agree
It's pretty. But what is it *for*?"

Morris Bishop

There was a young person called Smarty
Who sent out his cards for a party;
    So exclusive and few
    Were the friends that he knew
That no one was present but Smarty.

There was a young man, let me say,
Of West Pumpkinville, Maine, U.S.A.
    You tell me there's not
    Such a place? Thanks a lot.
I forget what he did anyway.

David McCord

A WARNING

I know a young girl who can speak
French, German, and Latin and Greek.
    I see her each day,
    And it grieves me to say
That her English is painfully weak!

Mary A. Webber

There was a young lady from Woosester
Who ussessed to crow like a roosester.
    She ussessed to climb
    Seven trees at a time—
But her sisester ussessed to boosester.

Said a lady beyond Pompton Lakes
"I do make such silly mistakes!
    Now the car's in the hall!
    It went right through the wall
When I mixed up the gas and the brakes."
Morris Bishop

There was an old lady named Carr
Who took the 3:3 to Forfar;
    For she said: "I conceive
    It is likely to leave
Far before the 4:4 to Forfar."

There once was a man who said, "How
Shall I manage to carry my cow?
    For if I should ask it
    To get in my basket,
'Twould make such a terrible row."

A MAN OF PENNANG

An honest old man of Pennang
once borrowed a friend's boomerang.
"I'll return it," he cried,
and he tried and he tried
—but it always came back to Pennang.

N. M. Bodecker

There was an old man of Khartoum
Who kept two tame sheep in his room:
"For," he said, "they remind me
Of one left behind me,
But I cannot remember of whom."

There was an old looney of Rhyme
Whose candor was simply sublime:
    When they asked, "Are you there?"
    He said, "Yes, but take care,
For I'm never 'all there' at a time!"

Said the crab: " 'Tis not beauty or birth
That is needed to conquer the earth.
    To win in life's fight,
    First be sure you are right,
Then go sidewise for all you are worth."

Oliver Herford

THE YAK

There was a most odious Yak
Who took only toads on his Back:
If you asked for a Ride
He would act very Snide,
And go humping off, yicketty-yak.

Theodore Roethke

Incidents and Accidents

There was a young farmer of Leeds
Who swallowed six packets of seeds.
    It soon came to pass
    He was covered with grass,
And he couldn't sit down for the weeds.

There once was a boy of Quebec
Who was buried in snow to his neck.
    When asked, "Are you frizz?"
    He replied, "Yes, I is,
But we don't call this cold in Quebec."

Rudyard Kipling

APRIL FOOL

At show-and-tell time yesterday
I brought my pet skunk. Sad to say,
  Though it had been well taught
  Not to spray, it forgot.
Now we can't use the schoolhouse till May.

John Ciardi

STICKY SITUATION

Muttered centipede Slither McGrew,
"What on earth can I possibly do?
  Here I'm late for a date
  And foot seventy-eight
Has some chewing gum stuck to its shoe!"

X. J. Kennedy

There once was a big rattlesnake
Who bought him a caraway cake.
    When they said, "You will share
    With your neighbors your fare,"
He said, "That's where you make a mistake!"

A skeleton once in Khartoum
Asked a spirit up into his room;
    They spent the whole night
    In the eeriest fight
As to which should be frightened of whom.

There once was a barber of Kew,
Who went very mad at the Zoo;
He tried to enamel
The face of the camel,
And gave the brown bear a shampoo.

Cosmo Monkhouse

A thrifty young fellow of Shoreham
Made brown paper trousers and woreham;
He looked nice and neat
Till he bent in the street
To pick up a pin; then he toreham.

Going home with her books through the snows,
Went Maude, when a blizzard arose.
Despite winter's blast,
Maude got home at last
But the books had no jackets and froze.

Wallace Tripp

There was once a most charming young miss
Who considered her ice-skating bliss;
But one day, alack!
Her skates, they were slack.
And she ended up something like this.

There was a young lady named Hannah,
Who slipped on a peel of banana.
    More stars she espied
    As she lay on her side
Than are found in the "Star-Spangled Banner."

Cries a sheep to a ship on the Amazon
(A Clipper sheep ship that her lamb is on),
    "Remember, dear Willy
    The nights will be chilly,
So keep your white woolly pajamas on!"

J. Patrick Lewis

There was a young lady of Spain
Who was dreadfully sick on a train,
Not once, but again
And again and again,
And again and again and again.

There was a young girl named O'Neill,
Who went up in the great Ferris wheel;
But when halfway around
She looked at the ground,
And it cost her an eighty-cent meal.

There was once a young man of Oporta
Who daily got shorter and shorter,
    The reason he said
    Was the hod on his head
Which was filled with the heaviest mortar.

Lewis Carroll

A small boy, while learning to swim,
Jumped into the water with vim.
    He lit on his sister,
    But wished he had missed her,
For it knocked all the breath out of him.

Elizabeth Gordon

There was a young man from the city,
Who met what he thought was a kitty;
    He gave it a pat,
    And said, "Nice little cat!"
And they buried his clothes out of pity.

A DRIVER FROM DEERING

A school bus driver from Deering
disconcertingly kept disappearing:
he would head for Cape May,
but end up in Bombay
—because something was wrong with the steering.

N. M. Bodecker

There was an old lady of Rye,
Who was baked by mistake in a pie;
    To the household's disgust
    She emerged through the crust,
And exclaimed, with a yawn, "Where am I?"

An obnoxious Old Person named Hackett
Bought a huge trunk and started to pack it.
    When he tripped and fell in it
    And it shut the next minute,
He proceeded to make quite a racket.

William Jay Smith

A mouse in her room woke Miss Dowd;
She was frightened and screamed very loud,
Then a happy thought hit her—
To scare off the critter,
She sat up in bed and meowed.

A PERSON IN SPAIN

An indignant young person in Spain
looked out at a gray, grimy rain
and cried: "Will you clear!
Who told *you* to come here?
You horrible **Old English Rain.**"

N. M. Bodecker

BE KIND TO DUMB ANIMALS

There once was an ape in a zoo
Who looked out through the bars and saw—YOU!
Do you think it's fair
To give poor apes a scare?
I think it's a mean thing to do!

John Ciardi

Peculiar People

A BRIGHT IDEA

A pretentious old man of the Bosporus
Used to cover his goat cart with phosphorus
    So that, driving by night
    He would get the green light
And his goats would consider him prosperous.

X. J. Kennedy

A MAN IN A TREE

A furious man in a tree
Said: "What's all this nature to me?
I have looked at the view.
Now what do I do?
I ought to have brung my TV."

N. M. Bodecker

A CRUSTY MECHANIC

There was an old crusty mechanic
Whose manners were fierce and tyrannic:
dull headlights would glare
At his furious stare,
—and dead engines turn over in panic!
N. M. Bodecker

There was a young lady of Crete,
Who was so exceedingly neat,
  When she got out of bed
  She stood on her head,
To make sure of not soiling her feet.

A certain young fellow, named Bobbie
Rode his steed back and forth in the lobby:
    When the clerk said: "Indoors
    Is no place for a horse"
He replied: "But, you see, it's my hobby."

There was a young lady named Ruth,
Who had a great passion for truth.
    She said she would die
    Before she would lie,
And she died in the prime of her youth.

MY SISTER

My sister's remarkably light,
She can float to a fabulous height.
It's a troublesome thing,
But we tie her with string,
And we use her instead of a kite.

Margaret Mahy

There was a young girl of Asturias,
Whose temper was frantic and furious.
  She used to throw eggs
  At her grandmother's legs—
A habit unpleasant, but curious.

A matron well known in Montclair
Was never quite sure what to wear.
    Once when very uncertain
    She put on a lace curtain
And ran a bell cord through her hair.

William Jay Smith

TENNIS CLINIC

There was a young man from Port Jervis
Who developed a marvelous service
But was sorry he learned it
For if someone returned it
It made him impossibly nervous.

Lillian Morrison

An impressionable lady in Wales
Had a passion for tragical tales;
    The torrents of tears
    That she wept through the years
They came and collected in pails.
Edward Gorey

There once was a person of Benin,
Who wore clothes not fit to be seen in;
    When told that he shouldn't
    He replied, "Gumscrumrudent!"—
A word of inscrutable meanin'!
Cosmo Monkhouse

A man who was fond of his skunk
Thought he smelled pure and pungent as punk.
But his friends cried No, no,
No, no, no, no, no, *no*!
He just stinks, or he stank, or he stunk.
David McCord

Said a restless young person of Yew,
"I will purchase a nice kangaroo;
I can sit in her pouch
And pretend it's a couch
And wherever she hops, I will too!"
Myra Cohn Livingston

An Old Man from Okefenokee
Liked to sing in a most dismal low key;
He would perch on a log
And boom like a frog
Through the dark swamp of Okefenokee.
William Jay Smith

There was a faith-healer of Deal
Who said, "Although pain isn't real,
If I sit on a pin
And I puncture my skin
I dislike what I *fancy* I feel!"

Said an Ogre from old Saratoga
I've tried to de-Ogre by Yoga
    I've stood on my head
    all day in my bed
but the mirror still says I'm an Ogre.
Conrad Aiken

Said old Peeping Tom of Fort Lee:
"Peeping ain't what it's cracked up to be;
    I lose all my sleep,
    And I peep and I peep,
And I find 'em all peeping at me."
Morris Bishop

There was an Old Man who said, "Well!
Will *nobody* answer this bell?
  I have pulled day and night,
  Till my hair has grown white.
But nobody answers this bell!"

Edward Lear

There was a young lady of Ealing,
Who had a peculiar feeling
  That she was a fly,
  And wanted to try
To walk upside down on the ceiling.

There was a Young Lady of Norway,
Who casually sat in a doorway;
    When the door squeezed her flat,
    She exclaimed, "What of that?"
This courageous Young Lady of Norway.
Edward Lear

There once was a girl of New York
Whose body was lighter than cork;
    She had to be fed
    For six weeks upon lead
Before she went out for a walk.
Cosmo Monkhouse

There was, in the village of Patton,
A chap who at church kept his hat on.
    "If I wake up," he said,
    "With my hat on my head,
I'll know that it hasn't been sat on."

SOMETIMES EVEN PARENTS WIN

There was a young lady from Gloucester
Who complained that her parents both bossed her,
    So she ran off to Maine.
    Did her parents complain?
Not at all—they were glad to have lost her.

John Ciardi

Strange Shapes

There was an Old Lady named Hart,
Whose appearance gave people a start:
    Her shape was a candle's
    Her ears like door handles,
And her front teeth three inches apart.
William Jay Smith

There was a young lady of Lynn
Who was so excessively thin
    That when she essayed
    To drink lemonade
She slipped through the straw and fell in.

There was an old maid of Berlin,
Who was most distressingly thin,
    She was locked out one day,
    But the neighbors all say,
She pushed out the key and crawled in.

Elizabeth Gordon

There was an old fellow named Green,
Who grew so abnormally lean,
    And flat, and compressed,
    That his back touched his chest,
And sideways he couldn't be seen.

A small mouse in Middleton Stoney
Grew pitifully skinny and bony;
    "It's apparent," he said,
    "I'm improperly fed
On a diet of raw macaroni."
Myra Cohn Livingston

There was a young lady named Flo,
Who was fat as a capital O;
    When the people said, "Why
    Is this thus?" she'd reply,
"I suppose it's the way that I grow."

K is for plump little Kate,
Who's handicapped sadly by weight.
  When we send her away
  For a visit we say,
" 'Twill be cheaper to send her by freight."

Wailed a ghost in a graveyard at Kew,
"Oh my friends are so fleeting and few,
  For it's gravely apparent
  That if you're transparent
There is no one who knows if it's *you*!"

Myra Cohn Livingston

There was a young damsel of Lynn
Whose waist was so charmingly thin,
    The dressmaker needed
    A microscope—she did—
To fit this slim person of Lynn.

There was an old man of the Cape
Who made himself garments of crepe.
    When asked, "Do they tear?"
    He replied, "Here and there;
But they're perfectly splendid for shape."
Robert Louis Stevenson

A PERSONAL EXPERIENCE

A puppy whose hair was so flowing
There really was no means of knowing
    Which end was his head
    Once stopped me and said,
"Please, sir, am I coming or going?"
Oliver Herford

There was a small maiden named Maggie,
Whose dog was enormous and shaggy,
    The front end of him
    Looked vicious and grim—
But the tail end was friendly and waggy.

There was a young angler of Worthing,
Who dug up ten worms and a fur thing.
    He said, "How I wish
    Eleven fine fish
Would snap up these things I'm unearthing."

There was once a young fellow of Wall
Who grew up so gigantically tall
    That his friends dug a pit
    Where he'd comfortably sit
When he wished to converse with them all.

Myra Cohn Livingston

There once was a centipede neat,
Who bought shoes for all of his feet;
    "For," he said, "I might chance
    To go to a dance,
And I must have my outfit complete."

There once was an old kangaroo,
Who painted his children sky-blue;
    When his wife said, "My dear,
    Don't you think they look queer?"
He replied, "I don't know but they do."

An Elephant sat on some kegs
And juggled glass bottles and eggs,
    And he said, "I surmise
    This occasions surprise,—
But, oh dear, how it tires one's legs!"

J. G. Francis

There was a young man of St. Kitts,
Who was very much troubled with fits;
    The eclipse of the moon
    Threw him into a swoon;
When he tumbled and broke into bits.

There was an old man of the Nore,
The same shape behind as before.
    They did not know where
    To offer a chair,
So he had to sit down on the floor.

All in the Head

As a beauty I'm not a great star,
There are others more handsome by far,
    But my face, I don't mind it,
    Because I'm behind it—
'Tis the folks in the front that I jar.

Anthony Euwer

There was an old man of Blackheath,
Who sat on his set of false teeth.
    Said he, with a start,
    "O Lord, bless my heart!
I've bitten myself underneath!"

There was an old man of Tarentum,
Who gnashed his false teeth till he bent 'em.
    When they asked him the cost
    Of what he had lost,
He replied, "I can't say, for I rent 'em."

There was an Old Man from Luray
Who always had something to say;
    But each time he tried
    With his mouth opened wide
His big tongue would get in the way.
William Jay Smith

No matter how grouchy you're feeling,
You'll find the smile more or less healing.
    It grows in a wreath
    All around the front teeth—
Thus preserving the face from congealing.
Anthony Euwer

There was a Young Lady named Rose
Who was constantly blowing her nose;
    Because of this failing
    They sent her off whaling
So the whalers could say: "Thar she blows!"
William Jay Smith

There was a young lady of Kent,
Whose nose was most awfully bent.
    One day, I suppose,
    She followed her nose,
For no one knew which way she went.

There was a Young Lady whose nose
Was so long that it reached to her toes;
    So she hired an Old Lady,
    Whose conduct was steady,
To carry that wonderful nose.

Edward Lear

There was a young lady of Firle,
Whose hair was addicted to curl;
    It curled up a tree,
    And all over the sea,
That expansive young lady of Firle.
Edward Lear

I'd rather have fingers than toes;
I'd rather have ears than a nose;
    And as for my hair,
    I'm glad that it's there.
I'll be awfully sad when it goes.
Gelett Burgess

A PERSON IN STIRLING

A silly young person in Stirling
desired her hair to be curling.
Despite curlers and creams
it got straighter, it seems
—but her nose started twisting and twirling.

N. M. Bodecker

There was an Old Person of Dutton,
Whose head was as small as a button;
So to make it look big
He purchased a wig,
And rapidly rushed about Dutton.

Edward Lear

From Number Nine, Penwiper Mews,
There is really abominable news:
  They've discovered a head
  In the box for the bread
But nobody seems to know whose.

Edward Gorey

There was an Old Man with a beard,
Who said, "It is just as I feared!—
  Two Owls and a Hen,
  Four Larks and a Wren,
Have all built their nests in my beard."

Edward Lear

There was a young man of Devizes,
Whose ears were of different sizes;
The one that was small
Was of no use at all,
But the other won several prizes.

There was a young maid who said, "Why
Can't I look in my ear with my eye?
If I give my mind to it,
I'm sure I can do it.
You never can tell till you try."

There was a young fellow named Shear
Who stuck a ball-point in his ear.
    As he punctured the drum
    He said, "That hurts some,
But the rest of the way through is clear."
John Ciardi

There once was a dancing black bear
Who, instead of a hat, wore a pair
    Of shoes on his head.
    "It's a two-step," he said,
"And it feels like I'm walking on air."
J. Patrick Lewis

Fabulous Foods

A LADY IN MADRID

A lady who lived in Madrid
made soup a way no one else did:
she swallowed some broth
with some herbs wrapped in a cloth,
and covered her head with a lid.

N. M. Bodecker

An epicure, dining at Crewe,
Found quite a large mouse in his stew.
    Said the waiter, "Don't shout
    And wave it about
Or the rest will be wanting one too."

ARTHUR

There was an old man of Calcutta,
Who coated his tonsils with butta,
    Thus converting his snore
    From a thunderous roar
To a soft, oleaginous mutta.

Ogden Nash

There was a young prince in Bombay,
Who always would have his own way;
    He pampered his horses
    On five or six courses,
Himself eating nothing but hay.

Walter Parke

A discerning young lamb of Long Sutton
Begged his grandfather, "Don't be a glutton;
    For you eat up the grass
    In a manner so crass
That they'll soon have you carved up as mutton."
Myra Cohn Livingston

There was a young man of Bengal
Who went to a fancy-dress ball,
    He went, just for fun,
    Dressed up as a bun,
And a dog ate him up in the hall.

They tell of a hunter named Shephard
Who was eaten for lunch by a lephard.
    Said the lephard, "Egad!
    You'd be tastier, lad,
If you had been salted and pephard."

Said Gus Goop, "That spaghetti was great!
Only—where in the world is my plate?
    Something hard as a bullet
    Feels stuck in my gullet—
Could it be that canned tuna I ate?"

X. J. Kennedy

THE PROVIDENT PUFFIN

There once was a provident puffin
Who ate all the fish he could stuff in.
    Said he, " 'Tis my plan
    To eat when I can:
When there's nuffin' to eat I eat nuffin'."

Oliver Herford

A PROFESSOR CALLED CHESTERTON

There was a professor called Chesterton,
Who went for a walk with his best shirt on.
    Being hungry he ate it,
    But lived to regret it,
As it ruined for life his digesterton.

W. S. Gilbert

There was a young pig who, in bed,
Nightly slumbered with eggs on his head.
When the sun at its rise
Made him open his eyes,
He enjoyed a quick breakfast in bed.

Arnold Lobel

There was an old man from the Rhine
Who was asked at what hour he would dine.
He replied, "At eleven,
At three, six, and seven,
At eight and a quarter of nine."

There was a young lady named Perkins,
Who had a great fondness for gherkins;
    She went to a tea
    And ate twenty-three,
Which pickled her internal workin's.

There was a young man so benighted,
He never knew when he was slighted.
    He went to a party,
    And ate just as hearty
As if he'd been really invited.

There was a sad pig with a tail
Not curly, but straight as a nail.
So he ate simply oodles
Of pretzels and noodles
Which put a fine twist to his tail.

Arnold Lobel

There was a fat lady from Eye
Who felt she was likely to die;
But for fear that once dead
She would not be well-fed,
She gulped down a pig, a cow, a sheep, twelve buns, a seven-layer cake, four cups of coffee, and a green apple pie.

There was an old person of Dean
Who dined on one pea, and one bean;
For he said, "More than that
Would make me too fat."
That cautious old person of Dean.

Edward Lear

There was an old person of Leeds,
And simple indeed were his needs.
Said he: "To save toil
Growing things in the soil,
I'll just eat the packets of seeds!"

THE UNFORTUNATE GIRAFFE

There was once a giraffe who said, "What
Do I want with my tea strong or hot?
For my throat's such a length
The tea loses its strength,
And is cold ere it reaches the spot."

Oliver Herford

Odd Numbers and Outer Space

IT CAME FROM OUTER SPACE

There once was a Martian named Zed
With antennae all over his head.
    He sent out a lot
    Of di-di-dash-dot
But nobody knows what he said.

John Ciardi

Doctor Who, I am forced to admit,
Is a booby, a crackpot, a twit.
    Other Time Lords all laugh
    When he trips on his scarf
That took X plus Y light years to knit.

Charles Connell

A scientist living at Staines
Is searching with infinite pains
    For a new type of sound
    Which he hopes, when it's found,
Will travel much faster than planes.
R. J. P. Hewison

A Martian named Harrison Harris
Decided he'd like to see Paris;
    In space (so we learn)
    He forgot where to turn—
And that's why he's now on Polaris.
Al Graham

A luckless time-traveler from Lynn
Leaned too close for a look and fell in
    To a puddle of slime
    On the first day of time
And so, naturally, couldn't have been.

X. J. Kennedy

There was a young lady named Bright,
Who traveled much faster than light.
    She started one day
    In a relative way,
And returned on the previous night.

Said the condor, in tones of despair:
"Not even the atmosphere's rare.
    Since man took to flying,
    It's really *too* trying,
The people one meets in the air."

Oliver Herford

Young Frankenstein's robot invention
Caused trouble too awful to mention.
    Its actions were ghoulish,
    Which proves it is foolish
To monkey with Nature's intention.

Berton Braley

There was an Old Man of the Hague,
Whose ideas were excessively vague;
He built a balloon,
To examine the moon,
That deluded Old Man of the Hague.

Edward Lear

There was an old man who said, "Do
Tell me *how* I should add two and two?
I think more and more
That it makes about four—
But I fear that is almost too few."

There was an old man who said, "Gee!
I can't multiply seven by three!
    Though fourteen seems plenty,
    It might come to twenty—
I haven't the slightest idee!"

'Tis a favorite project of mine
A new value of *pi* to assign.
    I would fix it at 3
    For it's simpler, you see,
Than 3 point 1 4 1 5 9.

Harvey L. Carter

Cried a man on the Salisbury Plain
"Don't disturb me—I'm counting the rain;
    Should you cause me to stop
    I might miss half-a-drop
And would have to start over again."

Myra Cohn Livingston

PHILANDER

A Man named Philander S. Goo
Said, "I *know* my Legs Add up to Two!
But I count up to One,
And I think I am Done!—
Oh What! Oh what what can I DO?"

Theodore Roethke

There was an old fellow of Trinity
Who solved the square root of Infinity,
    But it gave him such fidgets
    To count up the digits,
He chucked Math and took up Divinity.

LET X EQUAL HALF

A mathematician named Bath
Let x equal half that he hath.
    He gave away y
    Then sat down to pi
And choked. What a sad after*math*.

J. F. Wilson

A mathematician named Lynch
To a centipede said, "It's a cinch;
    With your legs I've reckoned,
    That I'll know in a second,
Just how many feet in an inch."

A bridge engineer, Mister Crumpett,
Built a bridge for the good River Bumpett.
    A mistake in the plan
    Left a gap in the span,
But he said, "Well, they'll just have to jump it."

Said Mrs. Isosceles Tri,
"That I'm sharp I've no wish to deny;
  But I do not dare
  To be perfectly square—
I'm sure if I did I should die!"
Clinton Brooks Burgess

Said Rev. Rectangular Square,
"To say that I'm *lost* is not fair;
  For, though you have found
  That I never am round,
You knew all the time I was there."
Clinton Brooks Burgess

Flutes and Fiddles

An extinct old ichthyosaurus
Once offered to sing in a chorus;
    But the rest of the choir
    Were obliged to retire,
His voice was so worn and sonorous.

There was an old person of Tring
Who, when somebody asked her to sing,
    Replied, "Isn't it odd?
    I can never tell 'God
Save the Weasel' from 'Pop Goes the
  King'!"

There were three little birds in a wood,
Who always sang hymns when they could.
    What the words were about
    They could never make out,
But they felt it was doing them good!

An opera star named Maria
Always tried to sing higher and higher,
    Till she hit a high note
    Which got stuck in her throat—
Then she entered the Heavenly Choir.

There was an Old Man of the Isles,
Whose face was pervaded with smiles;
    He sang "Hum dum diddle,"
    And played on the fiddle,
That amiable Man of the Isles.

Edward Lear

"Now just who," muses Uncle Bill Biddle,
"Drilled a dreadful big hole through my fiddle?
    When I play a folk air
    Air is all there is there
And my tune comes out minus its middle."

X. J. Kennedy

There was an Old Man with a gong,
Who bumped at it all the day long;
    But they called out, "Oh law!
    You're a horrid old bore!"
So they smashed that Old Man with a gong.

Edward Lear

There was a Young Lady of Tyre,
Who swept the loud chords of a lyre;
    At the sound of each sweep
    She enraptured the deep,
And enchanted the city of Tyre.

Edward Lear

There was a Young Lady whose chin
Resembled the point of a pin;
    So she had it made sharp,
    And purchased a harp,
And played several tunes with her chin.

Edward Lear

A boy who played tunes on a comb,
Had become such a nuisance at homb,
    That ma spanked him, and then—
    "Will you do it again?"
And he cheerfully answered her, "Nomb."

A bugler named Dougal MacDougal
Found ingenious ways to be frugal.
    He learned how to sneeze
    In various keys,
Thus saving the price of a bugle.

Ogden Nash

A tutor who tooted the flute
Tried to tutor two tooters to toot,
    Said the two to the tutor,
    "Is it harder to toot or
To tutor two tooters to toot?"

There was a Young Lady of Bute,
Who played on a silver-gilt flute;
  She played several jigs
  To her Uncle's white Pigs:
That amusing Young Lady of Bute.
Edward Lear

There was a young pig from Chanute
Who could pipe little songs on a flute.
When she practiced her scales,
A large crowd of snails
Came to listen, enrapt in Chanute.
Arnold Lobel

A farmer in Knox, Ind.,
Had a daughter he called Mar.
    But the neighbors said "O,
    We really must go,"
Whenever she played the p.

There was a young lady of Rio,
Who essayed to take part in a trio;
    But her skill was so scanty
    She played it andante
Instead of allegro con brio!

Wordplay and Puns

PITCHER McDOWELL

A farm team pitcher, McDowell,
pitched an egg at a batter named Owl.
They cried: "Get a hit!"
But it hatched in the mitt
—and the umpire called it a "fowl!"

N. M. Bodecker

Once a grasshopper (food being scant)
Begged an ant some assistance to grant;
    But the ant shook his head,
    "I can't help you," he said,
"It's an uncle you need, not an ant."

Oliver Herford

A handsome young noble of Spain
Met a lion one day in the rain.
    He ran in a fright
    With all of his might,
But the lion, he ran with his mane!

A father once said to his son,
"The next time you make up a pun,
    Go out in the yard
    And kick yourself hard,
And I will begin when you've done."

A maiden caught stealing a dahlia,
Said, "Oh, you shan't tell on me, shahlia?"
    But the florist was hot,
    And he said, "Like as not
They'll send you to jail, you bad gahlia."

A barber who lived in Batavia
Was known for his fearless behavia.
    An enormous baboon
    Broke in his saloon,
But he murmured, "I'm blamed if I'll shavia."

A beautiful lady named Psyche
Is loved by a fellow named Yche.
    One thing about Ych
    The lady can't lych
Is his beard, which is dreadfully spyche.

A Boston boy went out to Yuma
And there he encountered a puma—
    And later they found
    Just a spot on the ground,
And a puma in very good huma.
            D. D. (in Boston Transcript*)*

There's a girl out in Ann Arbor, Mich.,
To meet whom I never would wich.,
    She'd eat up ice cream
    Till with colic she'd scream,
Then order another big dich.

There was a young maiden called Eighmy,
Who was a good girl all the seighmy.
    At nine every night
    She'd kneel and recight
A little verse called "Now I leighmy."

An unpopular youth of Cologne,
With a pain in his stomach did mogne.
He heaved a great sigh
And said, "I would digh,
But the loss would be only my ogne."

An old couple living in Gloucester
Had a beautiful girl, but they loucester;
She fell from a yacht,
And never the spacht
Could be found where the cold waves had toucester.

A rather polite man of Hawarden,
When taking a walk in his gawarden,
    If he trod on a slug,
    A worm or a bug,
Would say, "My dear friend, I beg pawarden!"

A painter who came from Great Britain
Hailed a lady who sat with her knitain.
    He remarked with a sigh,
    "That park bench—well, I
Just painted it, right where you're sitain."

A girl, who weighed many an oz.
Used language I dared not pronoz.
    For a fellow unkind
    Pulled her chair out behind
Just to see (so he said) if she'd boz.

A lady who lived in Mont.
Had a beautiful daughter named H.,
    Who once took a seat
    On Twentieth Street,
Having slipped on a piece of ban.

A flea and a fly in a flue
Were imprisoned, so what could they do?
    Said the fly, "Let us flee."
    Said the flea, "Let us fly."
So they flew through a flaw in the flue.

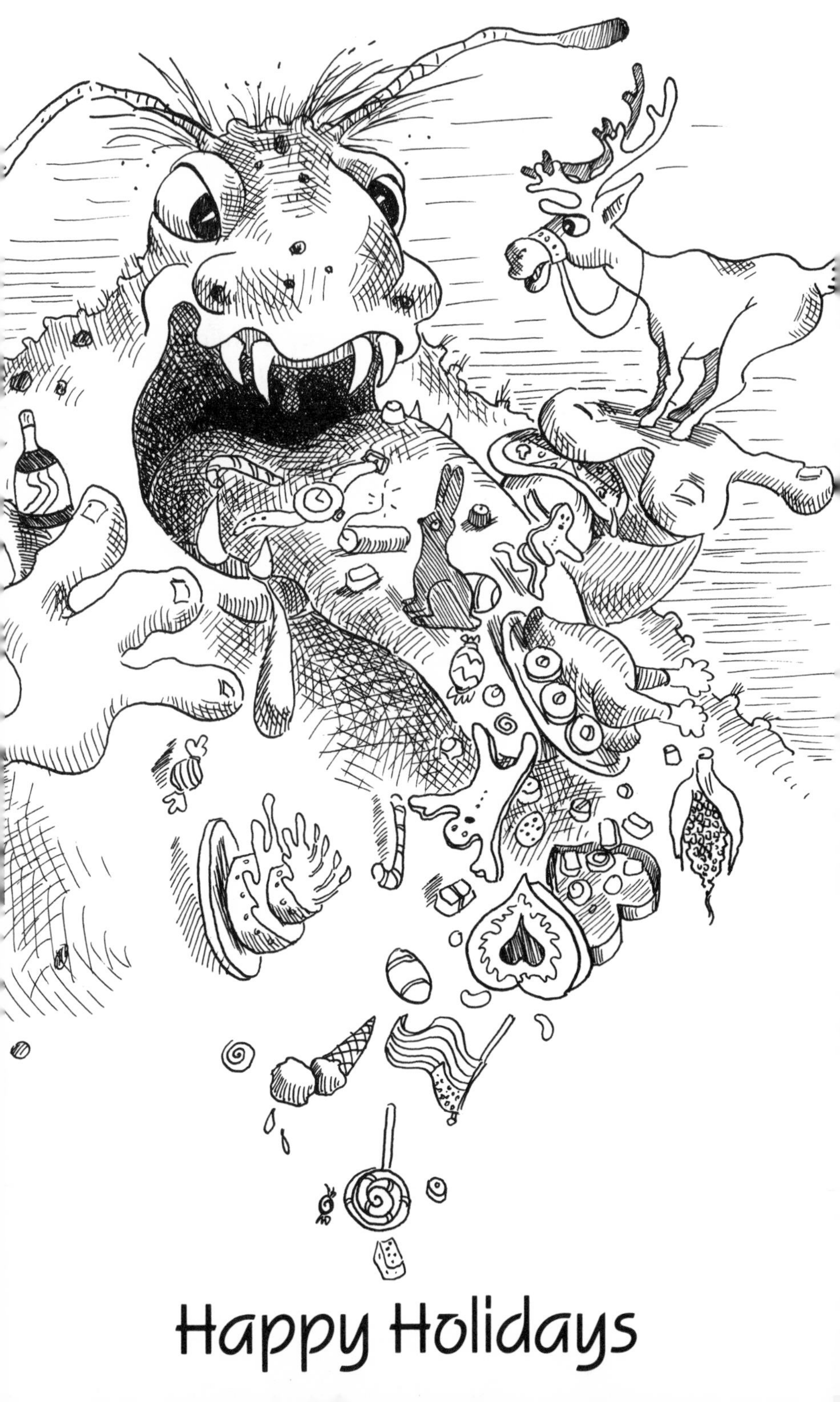
Happy Holidays

A fellow named Percival Stein
Sent Zelda a large valentine.
    Cried Zelda, "It's clever
    But never—oh never
Could someone named Percy be mine!"

R. H. Marks

A silly young fellow named Ben
Swallowed his wrist watch, and then
    He coughed up the date
    And the time on his plate—
April first, twenty seconds past ten.

Jack Prelutsky

I've drowned seventy ants in a pool,
I've burned down five rooms of the school,
    I've stolen six pies
    And told terrible lies
But they'll never catch this April Fool!

Ann Story

It's neither amusing nor funny
To feel any love for a bunny
    Who hops all around
    Hiding eggs on the ground
When he skips me and never leaves unny.

R. H. Marks

FOURTH OF JULY

Hurrah for the Fourth of July
When fireworks burst in the sky!
    All you need is a match
    And a quick little scratch
And a rocket and fuse and______GOOD-BYE

Myra Cohn Livingston

THE HALLOWEEN HOUSE

I'm told there's a Green Thing in there.
And the sign on the gate says BEWARE!
    But of course it's not true.
    That's why I'm sending you
To sneak in and find out—*but take care*!

John Ciardi

SAID THE MONSTER

Said the Monster, "You all think that I
Love to lunch on the folks who go by.
  If only you knew
  I'd much rather chew
On a peppery cheese pizza pie!"

Lilian Moore

The Pilgrims ate quahaugs and corn yet,
Which gourmets would scorn through a lorgnette.
  For this kind of living
  They proclaimed a Thanksgiving.
I'm thankful I hadn't been born yet.

Ogden Nash

AN ODD ONE

There once was a finicky ocelot
Who all the year round was cross a lot
Except at Thanksgiving
When he enjoyed living
For he liked to eat cranberry sauce a lot.

Eve Merriam

There is a young reindeer named Donder,
Of whom Santa couldn't be fonder;
    But he falls off the roofs
    When his four little hoofs
Impatiently cause him to wander.

J. Patrick Lewis

A woman named Mrs. S. Claus
Deserves to be heard from because
    She sits in her den
    Baking gingerbread men
While her husband gets all the applause.

J. Patrick Lewis

The Very End

A careless zookeeper named Blake
Fell into a tropical lake.
    Said a fat alligator
    A few minutes later,
"Very nice, but I still prefer steak."

A certain young man of great gumption,
Among cannibals had the presumption
    To go—but, alack!
    He never came back.
They say 'twas a case of consumption.

A collegiate damsel named Breeze,
Weighed down by B.A.'s and Litt. D.'s,
  Collapsed from the strain.
  Alas, it was plain
She was killing herself—by degrees.

A daring young lady of Guam
Observed, "The Pacific's so calm
  I'll swim out for a lark."
  She met a large shark . . .
Let us now sing the Ninetieth Psalm.

A decrepit old gasman, named Peter,
While hunting around for the meter,
Touched a leak with his light;
He rose out of sight—
And, as anyone who knows anything about poetry can tell you, he also ruined the meter.

A sea-serpent saw a big tanker,
Bit a hole in her side and then sank her.
It swallowed the crew
In a minute or two,
And then picked its teeth with the anchor.

AN EXPLORER NAMED BLISS

An intrepid explorer named Bliss
fell into a gorge or abyss,
But remarked as he fell:
"Oh I might just as well
get to the bottom of this . . ."

N. M. Bodecker

On a day when the ocean was sharky
Archaeologist Arthur McLarky
For a quick dip dived in,
But along came a fin—
All they found was his shovel and car key.

Said a foolish young lady of Wales,
"A smell of escaped gas prevails."
  Then she searched with a light,
  And later that night
Was collected—in seventeen pails!
Langford Reed

There once was a man in the Moon,
But he got there a little too soon.
  Some others came later
  And fell down a crater—
When *was* it? Next August? Last June?
David McCord

There once was a man who said, "Why
Can't I look that big snake in the eye?"
The snake said, "You can,"
And he looked at the man.
('Most any last line will apply.)

There once was a plesiosaurus
Which lived when the earth was all porous.
But it fainted with shame
When it first heard its name,
And departed long ages before us.

There once was a scarecrow named Joel
Who couldn't scare crows, save his soel.
    But the crows put the scare
    Into Joel. He's not there
Any more. That's his hat on the poel.

David McCord

There once were two cats of Kilkenny,
Each thought there was one cat too many;
    So they fought and they fit,
    And they scratched and they bit,
Till instead of two cats there weren't any.

There was a young fellow named Hall
Who fell in the spring in the fall.
    'Twould have been a sad thing
    Had he died in the spring.
But he didn't—he died in the fall.

There was a Young Person named Crockett
Who attached himself to a rocket;
    He flew out through space
    At such a great pace
That his pants flew out of his pocket.

William Jay Smith

There was a young woman from Niger
Who rode on the back of a tiger.
    They returned from the ride
    With the lady inside
And a smile on the face of the tiger.

There was a young fellow named Weir,
Who hadn't an atom of fear;
    He indulged a desire
    To touch a live wire;
('Most any old line will do here!)

There was a Young Lady of Ryde
Who ate a green apple and died;
    The apple fermented
    Inside the lamented,
And made cider inside her inside.

There was an Old Lady named Crockett
Who went to put a plug in a socket;
    But her hands were so wet
    She flew up like a jet
And came roaring back down like a rocket!

William Jay Smith

When a jolly young fisher named Fisher
Went fishing for fish in a fissure,
    A fish, with a grin,
    Pulled the fisherman in.
Now they're fishing the fissure for Fisher.

INDEX OF AUTHORS

Aiken, Conrad, 36

Bishop, Morris, 8, 10, 36
Bodecker, N. M., 12, 24, 26, 28, 29, 57, 62, 94, 113
Braley, Berton, 75
Burgess, Clinton Brooks, 85
Burgess, Gelett, 5, 56

Carroll, Lewis, 23
Carter, Harvey L., 77
Ciardi, John, 6, 7, 17, 26, 39, 60, 72, 106, 120
Connell, Charles, 72

D. D., 97

Euwer, Anthony, 52, 54

Fatchen, Max, 7
Francis, J. G., 50

Gilbert, W. S., 66
Gordon, Elizabeth, 23, 43
Gorey, Edward, 33, 58
Graham, Al, 73

Herford, Oliver, 5, 13, 47, 66, 70, 75, 94
Hewison, R. J. P., 73

Kennedy, X. J., 17, 28, 65, 74, 86
Kipling, Rudyard, 16

Lear, Edward, 37, 38, 55, 56, 57, 58, 70, 76, 86, 87, 88, 90
Lewis, J. Patrick, 21, 60, 108
Livingston, Myra Cohn, 34, 44, 45, 48, 64, 78, 106
Lobel, Arnold, 67, 69, 90

Mahy, Margaret, 31
Marks, R. H., 104, 105
McCord, David, 5, 9, 34, 114, 116
Merriam, Eve, 108
Monkhouse, Cosmo, 19, 33, 38

Moore, Lilian, 107
Morrison, Lillian, 32

Nash, Ogden, 63, 89, 107

Parke, Walter, 63
Prelutsky, Jack, 104

Reed, Langford, 114
Roethke, Theodore, 13, 78

Smith, William Jay, 25, 32, 35, 42, 53, 54, 117, 119
Stevenson, Robert Louis, 46
Story, Ann, 105

Tripp, Wallace, 20

Webber, Mary A., 9
Wilson, J. F., 79

INDEX OF TITLES AND FIRST LINES

A barber who lived in Batavia 96
A beautiful lady named Psyche 97
A Boston boy went out to Yuma 97
A boy who played tunes on a comb, 88
A bridge engineer, Mister Crumpett, 80
A bugler named Dougal MacDougal 89
A careless zookeeper named Blake 110
A certain young fellow, named Bobbie 30
A certain young man of great gumption 110
A collegiate damsel named Breeze, 111
A daring young lady of Guam 111
A decrepit old gasman, named Peter, 112
A discerning young lamb of Long Sutton 64
A farm team pitcher, McDowell, 94
A farmer in Knox, Ind., 91
A father once said to his son, 95
A fellow named Percival Stein 104
A flea and a fly in a flue 101
A furious man in a tree 28
A girl, who weighed many an oz. 101
A handsome young noble of Spain 95
A lady who lived in Madrid 62
A lady who lived in Mont. 101
A luckless time-traveler from Lynn 74
A maiden caught stealing a dahlia, 96
A Man named Philander S. Goo 78
A man who was fond of his skunk 34
A Martian named Harrison Harris 73
A mathematician named Bath 79

A mathematician named Lynch 80
A matron well known in Montclair 32
A mouse in her room woke Miss Dowd; 26
A painter who came from Great Britain 100
A pretentious old man of the Bosporus 28
A puppy whose hair was so flowing 47
A rather polite man of Hawarden, 100
A school bus driver from Deering 24
A scientist living at Staines 73
A sea-serpent saw a big tanker, 112
A silly young fellow named Ben 104
A silly young person in Stirling 57
A skeleton once in Khartoum 18
A small boy, while learning to swim, 23
A small mouse in Middleton Stoney 44
A thrifty young fellow of Shoreham 19
A tutor who tooted the flute 89
A woman named Mrs. S. Claus 108
An Elephant sat on some kegs 50
An epicure, dining at Crewe, 62
An extinct old ichthyosaurus 84
An honest old man of Pennang 12
An impressionable lady in Wales 34
An indignant young person in Spain 26
An intrepid explorer named Bliss 113
An obnoxious Old Person named Hackett 25
An old couple living in Gloucester 99
An Old Man from Okefenokee 35
An opera star named Maria 85
An unpopular youth of Cologne, 99
APRIL FOOL 17

ARTHUR 63
As a beauty I'm not a great star, 52
At show-and-tell time yesterday 17

BE KIND TO DUMB ANIMALS 26
BRIGHT IDEA, A 28

Cried a man on the Salisbury Plain 78
Cries a sheep to a ship on the Amazon 21
CRUSTY MECHANIC, A 29

Doctor Who, I am forced to admit, 72
DRIVER FROM DEERING, A 24

EXPLORER NAMED BLISS, AN 113

FOURTH OF JULY 106
From Number Nine, Penwiper Mews, 58

GNAT AND THE GNU, THE 4
Going home with her books through the snows, 20

HALLOWEEN HOUSE, THE 106
"How absurd," said the gnat to the gnu, 4
Hurrah for the Fourth of July 106

I know a young girl who can speak 9
I wish that my room had a floor; 4
I'd rather have fingers than toes; 56
I'm told there's a Green Thing in there. 106
IT CAME FROM OUTER SPACE 72

It's neither amusing nor funny 105
I've drowned seventy ants in a pool, 105

K is for plump little Kate, 45
KEEPING BUSY IS BETTER THAN NOTHING 6

LADY IN MADRID, A 62
LET X EQUAL HALF 79

MAN IN A TREE, A 28
MAN OF PENNANG, A 12
Muttered centipede Slither McGrew, 18
MY SISTER 31
My sister's remarkably light, 31

No matter how grouchy you're feeling, 54
"Now just who," muses Uncle Bill Biddle, 86

ODD ONE, AN 108
On a day when the ocean was sharky 113
Once a grasshopper (food being scant) 94

PERSON IN SPAIN, A 26
PERSON IN STIRLING, A 57
PERSONAL EXPERIENCE, A 47
PHILANDER 78
PITCHER McDOWELL 94
PROFESSOR CALLED CHESTERTON, A 66
PROVIDENT PUFFIN, THE 66

Said a foolish young lady of Wales, 114

Said a lady beyond Pompton Lakes 10
Said a restless young person of Yew, 34
Said an Ogre from old Saratoga 36
Said Gus Goop, "That spaghetti was great! 65
Said Mrs. Isosceles Tri, 81
Said old Peeping Tom of Fort Lee: 36
Said Rev. Rectangular Square, 81
Said the condor, in tones of despair: 75
Said the crab: " 'Tis not beauty or birth 13
SAID THE MONSTER 107
Said the Monster, "You all think that I 107
SOMETIMES EVEN PARENTS WIN 39
STICKY SITUATION 18

TENNIS CLINIC 32
The Pilgrims ate quahaugs and corn yet, 107
There is a young reindeer named Donder, 108
There once was a barber of Kew 19
There once was a big rattlesnake 18
There once was a boy of Bagdad, 5
There once was a boy of Quebec 16
There once was a centipede neat, 49
There once was a dancing black bear 60
There once was a finicky ocelot 108
There once was a girl of New York 38
There once was a man in the Moon, 114
There once was a man who said, "How 11
There once was a man who said, "Why 115
There once was a Martian named Zed 72
There once was a person of Benin, 33
There once was a plesiosaurus 115

There once was a provident puffin 66
There once was a scarecrow named Joel 116
There once was an ape in a zoo 26
There once was an old kangaroo, 49
There once were two cats of Kilkenny, 116
There was a brave hunter named Paul 120
There was a faith-healer of Deal 35
There was a fat lady from Eye 69
There was a most odious Yak 13
There was a professor called Chesterton, 66
There was a sad pig with a tail 69
There was a small maiden named Maggie, 47
There was a young angler of Worthing, 48
There was a young bard of Japan 6
There was a young damsel of Lynn 46
There was a young farmer of Leeds 16
There was a young fellow called Hugh 7
There was a young fellow named Hall 117
There was a young fellow named Shear 60
There was a young fellow named Weir, 118
There was a young fellow who thought 7
There was a young girl named O'Neill, 22
There was a young girl of Asturias, 31
There was a young lady from Gloucester 39
There was a young lady from Woosester 10
There was a young lady named Bright, 74
There was a young lady named Flo, 44
There was a young lady named Hannah, 21
There was a young lady named Perkins, 68
There was a Young Lady named Rose 54
There was a young lady named Ruth, 30

There was a young lady named Sue 6
There was a Young Lady of Bute, 90
There was a young lady of Crete, 29
There was a young lady of Ealing, 37
There was a young lady of Firle, 56
There was a young lady of Kent, 55
There was a young lady of Lynn 42
There was a Young Lady of Norway, 38
There was a young lady of Rio, 91
There was a Young Lady of Ryde 119
There was a young lady of Spain 22
There was a Young Lady of Tyre, 87
There was a Young Lady whose chin 88
There was a Young Lady whose nose 55
There was a young maid who said, "Why 59
There was a young maiden called Eighmy, 98
There was a young man from Port Jervis 32
There was a young man from the city, 24
There was a young man, let me say, 9
There was a young man of Bengal 64
There was a young man of Devizes, 59
There was a young man of St. Kitts, 50
There was a young man so benighted, 68
There was a young person called Smarty 8
There was a Young Person named Crockett 117
There was a young pig from Chanute 90
There was a young pig who, in bed, 67
There was a young prince in Bombay, 63
There was a young woman from Niger 118
There was an old crusty mechanic 29
There was an old fellow named Green, 43

There was an old fellow of Trinity 79
There was an old lady named Carr 11
There was an Old Lady named Crockett 119
There was an Old Lady named Hart, 42
There was an old lady of Rye, 25
There was an old looney of Rhyme 13
There was an old maid of Berlin, 43
There was an Old Man from Luray 53
There was an old man from the Rhine 67
There was an old man of Blackheath, 52
There was an old man of Calcutta, 63
There was an old man of Khartoum 12
There was an old man of Tarentum, 53
There was an old man of the Cape 46
There was an Old Man of the Hague, 76
There was an Old Man of the Isles, 86
There was an old man of the Nore, 50
There was an old man who said, "Do 76
There was an old man who said, "Gee! 77
There was an Old Man who said, "Well! 37
There was an Old Man with a beard, 58
There was an Old Man with a gong, 87
There was an old person of Dean 70
There was an Old Person of Dutton, 57
There was an old person of Leeds, 70
There was an old person of Tring 84
There was, in the village of Patton, 39
There was once a giraffe who said, "What 70
There was once a most charming young miss 20
There was once a young fellow of Wall 48
There was once a young man of Oporta 23

There were three little birds in a wood, 85
There's a girl out in Ann Arbor, Mich., 98
There's a tiresome young man from Bay Shore; 8
They tell of a hunter named Shephard 65
THINKER, THE 7
"This season our tunnips was red 5
'Tis a favorite project of mine 77

UNFORTUNATE GIRAFFE, THE 70

Wailed a ghost in a graveyard at Kew, 45
WARNING, A 9
When a jolly young fisher named Fisher 120
WIN SOME, LOSE SOME 120

YAK, THE 13
Young Frankenstein's robot invention 75